DADDY SHARK
LOVES TO FART!

By Frank Maxwell
Illustrated by: Dora Laszlo

To my dad,
he always knew how to lighten my
day with a good joke.

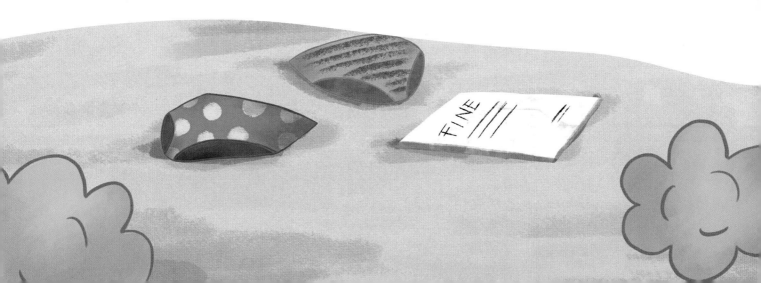

Hi, I'm **Sharky**,
and I'm a small shark.
I have to confess – I love to fart.

Do you think **Daddy Shark** disapproves of this?
Well, let me tell you about a habit of his.

We begin every morning with stretching in bed,
and suddenly, the whole room smells bad.

What does **Daddy** do?
He releases a fart or two.

Then we sit at the table and eat,
and suddenly, a "Puff" that doesn't smell sweet.

It comes from his bum,
and he does it all the time.

"Sharky, farting is good, don't hold it in.
Feel free to release gas," he says with a grin.
Puff, puff – he continues to fart.

"I proudly fart from the heart!"

Then we go swimming around,
and our farts abound!
We cause big waves,
and everyone complains!

We go to a restaurant to eat lunch.

We order beans and fruit punch.

Oh, dear! **Daddy** starts to fart straight away,

We go to the ocean market to buy some food, and of course, **Daddy Shark** is in a farting mood.

Puff, puff – the farts roar,

and they chase us out of the store.

Next, we head to the Ocean Zoo,
where Daddy lets out a fart or two.

Daddy Shark then takes me to school.
He leads me into the classroom.
Do you think that's cool?

Well, think twice;
What do you think he does?
In front of my teacher,
he farts just because.

We go to the small sharks' playground to play,
but all my friends immediately swim away.

I'm sure you know what causes that!

Daddy Shark farted while
I was having a chat.

Then off we go to the Adventure Park,
and there is a sign: It's forbidden to fart.

We hop on the rollercoaster,
and my **Daddy Shark** whispers,

"I think I have to toot
right now."

"Oh no, **Daddy Shark**, that's not allowed."

"But I can't hold it!"
So puff, puff he goes,
and everyone moans and holds their nose.

The rollercoaster stops,
the park officer arrives on the double.
He tells us to leave and not cause any more trouble.

Home we go, with a farting ticket and a fine to pay.

Dad grins, "It was worth it all the way!"

It starts getting hot; summer is near.
We need new bathing suits this year.

Our last ones fell apart,
from way too many farts.

We go into the ocean mall and try some suits on,
and **Daddy Shark** releases a
big fart from his bum.

The saleslady hears, and she goes nuts.

But what can we do? We love farts!

"Dad, I have to tell you something,
my rump hurts from farting.
I think we fart too much."
And he says,

HAPPY FATHER'S DAY,
Everyone!

Thank you for choosing my book; it means the world to me.

I want to offer you a free printable copy of my **DADDY SHARK COLORING AND ACTIVITY BOOK.**

FREEEEE GIFT FOR YOU!

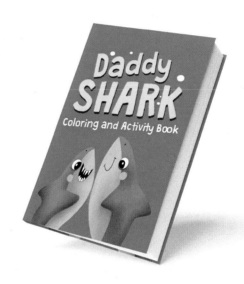

All you have to do is:

1. Solve the tricky maze (last page);
2. Take a picture of it;
3. Share it on your Instagram feed and tag me **@heyfrankmaxwell**;
4. You will get a unique link to download your free pdf.

Have a question? Let me know

Hello@frankmaxwell.com

ABOUT THE AUTHOR:

Teacher turned author and kids' mental health advocate. Frank is the author of the new children's book **Daddy Shark Loves to Fart!** Frank has given many workshops for parents and teachers on how to connect with kids through humor and storytelling.

A VERY VERYYY TRICKY MAZE!

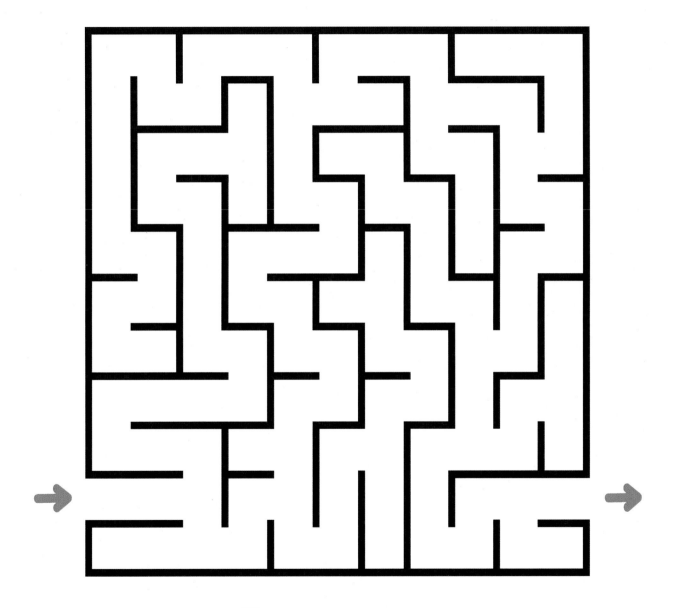

Made in the USA
Columbia, SC
17 June 2022

61837574R00022